Go Find Hanka!

GOLDEN GATE JUNIOR BOOKS
San Carlos • California

Weekly Reader Books presents

Go Find Hanka!

by Alexander L. Crosby

Drawings by Glen Rounds

With love to
HELEN PAPASHVILY
who lent me
Prairie and Rocky Mountain Adventures

Acknowledgement

This story of the prairie is based on the narrative of an anonymous hunter in *Prairie and Rocky Mountain Adventures, or, Life in the West*, by John C. Van Tramp, published at Columbus, Ohio, in 1868. The only names used in the original are those of the dog and the child.

THE MOST famous resident of Piatt County, Illinois, in the 1850s was a brown and white dog. Phil was known by name in every general store, and stories of his exploits had spread across the prairie to other counties.

"Why, that dog could find a prairie chicken ten feet down a gopher hole," one storekeeper told a visitor.

"Yup, and he'd climb a sycamore to point a wild turkey at the top," a local citizen added.

The facts are that not even a half-starved prairie chicken could squeeze into a gopher hole, and Phil had never got higher in a tree than his forepaws could reach. Yet the dog was able to do things that people could not understand, which is why he was credited with doing things he couldn't.

Phil was an English setter, the closest friend of Ralph Stark, a hunter who lived alone. The dog had a long nose, hazel eyes, silky ears, and a fringed tail that swung from side to side as he zigzagged through the prairie in search of plovers or prairie chickens.

He loved to hunt. Whenever Ralph took down his gun from the rack and slung his game bag over his shoulder, Phil went wild. He would upset the foot-stool and knock over the chair with his exuberant leaps. Once he toppled the wash stand. When they left the cabin, Phil's capers would become still wilder. He would make a mad dash at an invisible animal, barking furiously. Then he would run back to Ralph and roll over in the grass before tearing off again.

But as soon as the pair entered the prairie where game would be found, the dog became a different animal. There was no more barking or rollicking. Quietly and steadily Phil would trot back and forth in the deep

grass, always watching Ralph, always sniffing for prairie chickens or plovers.

Phil knew his work so well that he never wasted time following the trails of hawks or bitterns. But when he scented a prairie chicken his tail stopped swinging. He moved forward cautiously, step by step, until he could see the bird. Then he froze in a point—tail straight out, right foreleg raised and folded at the knee, every muscle as rigid as iron.

Ralph would come up, gun ready. The bird would take off at his approach. Aiming in a fraction of a second, the hunter would fire. Phil would go bounding off to retrieve the fallen bird. Ralph sold his game at the general store when the neighboring farmers were too busy in the fields to hunt for themselves.

There were many good hunting dogs on the Grand Prairie in the 1850s. Ralph believed that Phil was different because he was interested in more than hunting. The dog liked to watch caterpillars, spiders, and other small creatures. He was a careful observer when Ralph shaved or bathed, or when a friend stopped by for conversation. Sometimes he would sit quietly at night outside the cabin, listening to sounds from the dark and looking at the stars. The hunter used to say that his dog knew all of the principal constellations and never mistook a planet for a star.

Once, writing to a friend in the East, Ralph described Phil this way: "He has general intelligence. He is not merely a professor, he is a philosopher. He has ideas not pertaining to his own department of bird hunting."

A great test of the dog's understanding came, unexpectedly, early one summer morning. Ralph was asleep in his cabin on the edge of the Grand Prairie, and the black sky was flecked with stars. In another hour the robins would begin their early chorus in the garden of Indian corn, potatoes, turnips, and onions. Ralph had no affection for the rich prairie soil, for he would rather use a gun than a spade. But he liked to eat something beside prairie chicken, plover, rabbit, and venison, so he had dug up the thick-rooted prairie grass to make room for vegetables.

A growl from Phil made Ralph open his eyes. The setter was standing near the door. A few moments later a fist was thumping on the rough boards.

"Mr. Stark! Mr. Stark!" came an anxious cry. The voice was clearly a woman's.

Astonished by having a visitor before daylight, Ralph sprang from his bunk and pulled on a coat. He lit a candle, opened the door, and recognized Elsa Kleinsinger. She was the young wife of a German immigrant who had a farm three miles to the south.

Ralph remembered her long blonde hair, neatly braided and coiled around her head, and her deep blue eyes, serious and questioning. But now, as the young man quickly noticed, her hair was in disorder, her eyes were desperate.

"Mrs. Kleinsinger!" he cried. "What brings you here?"

Her words came as if her breath were gone. "Oh, my God! My little boy Hanka—he is lost in the prairie!"

"Lost? How long?"

"Ever since yesterday noon. My husband and I have searched all night. Mr. Stark, you think your dog could find him?"

Phil had been standing at Ralph's side, puzzled by having a visitor at this hour. He looked up at Ralph when he saw that the young mother was turning to him.

The hunter was silent. He knew the prairie and he knew his dog. There was no hope. A setter trained to find prairie chickens could not trail a five-year-old boy.

"Phil is a bird dog," Ralph finally said. "You need a bloodhound. It takes a bloodhound to follow the scent of a person."

"Where can I find a bloodhound?"

"I don't know of any around here," Ralph had to say.

"If there is no bloodhound, then we must try Phil," she urged. "You remember the time I showed you where a wild turkey had crossed a trail? You called Phil and he followed the turkey's spoor."

Mrs. Kleinsinger's words came tumbling out. "And when he got to the little stream the turkey had flown over he ran up and down the bank. Then he swam across and smelled all along the other bank until he found the trail again. He came up to the turkey and you shot it."

"Yes, I remember," said Ralph. "But Phil has been following the scent of birds all his life. Birds smell different from children."

Mrs. Kleinsinger was close to tears.

"Mr. Stark, your dog can follow the tracks of the snipe and the plover. They have such little feet! Think how big are the feet of Hanka. Surely Phil can follow his trail."

Ralph knew that a dog depends on his nose, not his eyes, to follow a track. He looked beyond the slender young woman to the endless dark of the prairie. It was a black ocean of grass, from two to six feet high, stretching farther than an Indian could run in a week. There was not a speck of bare earth,

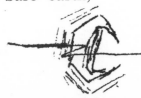

except for a network of trails left by the vanished buffalo and Indians. One trail might lead to a settlement. A dozen others would lead a wanderer deeper into the tall, waving grass.

The prairie had many low ridges of two to ten yards in height, like the swells of the ocean. But the grassy elevations all looked the same. There were no clusters of trees, no outcroppings of rock.

In the late spring the prairie blazed with wild flowers. In the late summer it often blazed with fires that blackened the ground as fast as the wind blew. Thousands of deer, wolves, rabbits, prairie chickens, and other birds had to run or fly for their lives.

There were no wagon roads and no fences. There was not a single landmark to guide a traveler. Only two weeks before, Ralph had found himself hopelessly lost on the prairie. He had walked for almost three hours, trying one trail after another. The late afternoon sun could not guide him because it was hidden by clouds. Finally he had sat down and waited for darkness, hoping that some stars could be seen. He was lucky. The skies cleared, revealing the Great Dipper and the Pole Star. He took a trail to the north and found his cabin only half a mile away.

A child lost in the prairie was almost certain to die.

Within the past two years two young children had wandered away from their cabins in the cultivated fields. Searchers found the skeleton of one who had been devoured by wolves. The other was never seen again.

These thoughts ran through Ralph's mind as he faced the terrified mother. He had no heart to tell her she would probably never touch Hanka's yellow curls again. A five-year-old boy could not see above most of the grass. Even if he could, there would be nothing to see but more grass, for miles and miles. And if he tried to follow an old trail he had only the faintest chance of reaching a cabin.

Mrs. Kleinsinger began again. "I left Hanka at the cabin yesterday noon when I carried dinner to the men working on the prairie. He was playing by the door, making little paths with a block of wood. When I came back he was gone."

Phil was listening to the man and the woman, turning his head from one to the other as they spoke. Now he looked up at Ralph expectantly.

There was only one thing to say, and Ralph hesitated no longer.

"Mrs. Kleinsinger, I don't think Phil can follow Hanka's trail—but we'll try. Just give me a few minutes to put on my clothes."

Stepping back into the cabin, Ralph threw off his coat, doused his face with water from a tin basin, then pulled on his clothes. He took down his gun from two pegs in the wall and walked out. Phil jumped after him, tail swinging. Could it be a hunt for prairie chickens in the dark?

Elsa led the way to her cabin, half-running. Although Ralph was fresh from a night's sleep, he had to push to keep up with her.

The young mother told more as they hurried along the rough path.

"I ran into the prairie and called to Hanka," she said. "He did not answer. But my husband heard me from the field and he came with the men. They went over the prairie in different directions, all of them shouting. Then some of the neighbors came to help us. But we did not hear Hanka's voice."

"How long did you keep hunting?"

"The neighbors went home as it grew dark. They had to care for their own children, but they said they will come back this morning. My husband made a great bonfire in our yard. He thought Hanka might

see it. Then we went into the prairie again, shouting and shouting. The noise might scare away wolves, yes?"

"Yes, it could," Ralph said, though he had doubts.

"So we stayed in the prairie, making a big noise, until I started for your cabin."

The first light of morning gave Ralph a good view of the Kleinsingers' tiny cabin which stood where the cultivated fields ended and the prairie began. To the north and east the open fields were dotted with the houses of other settlers. To the west and south the prairie stretched without limit.

The Kleinsinger cabin was built of boards and had only a single window. Great chunks of prairie turf, a foot thick, had been stacked as high as the window to keep out the raging winds of winter. A sluggish stream ran through a swampy area south of the house. Near the stream a well had been dug, and the path between house and well was packed hard. A wagon, a plow, and a few farm tools were scattered in the yard. There was a small shed with stalls for two horses.

Since Hanka's trail was already eighteen hours old, no time could be lost. Ralph had to teach his setter how to be a bloodhound in one short lesson. The place to begin was inside the cabin where Hanka slept and dressed.

The man and dog followed Elsa into the single room which was scantily equipped with furniture and food. The parents slept in a bunk made from rough boards, covered with a calico quilt. Hanka's trundle bed had been pushed out of the way beneath the bunk. A small table with a bench stood against one wall and a cast-iron stove was in a corner. Dishes and some tins of flour, sugar, coffee, and tea were arranged on two open shelves. The family's clothing hung on pegs, although a few treasured garments were kept in a battered old trunk that served as a stand for the wash basin.

"Let me have some of Hanka's clothing that hasn't been washed," Ralph said as he took off his hunting coat and put his gun in a corner. Mrs. Kleinsinger rummaged in a hamper and handed over a pair of trousers and a pair of socks. Ralph stowed the socks in a pocket and held out the trousers to his dog.

"Smell these, Phil," he said. "Smell. Hanka's trousers. Go find Hanka!"

Phil listened politely, sniffed obediently, and then looked toward the gun. Plainly, he was not interested in a pair of dirty trousers.

Ralph held out the trousers again. "Hanka's trousers. Go find Hanka!"

Phil looked up, bewildered. His master was acting quite peculiarly.

"Come, Phil, we are going to the prairie to find Hanka," Ralph said, walking to the door. The dog followed, pausing outside to sniff at the child's wooden shoes. But it was just a sniff of curiosity, not the serious effort of a bloodhound.

Already Ralph had decided on his strategy. It would be impossible to pick up Hanka's scent around the yard after eighteen hours. Smells did not last long on dirt, especially when many other feet had blurred the faint odor that a dog seeks. The only chance was to strike into the prairie where there might be a fresher scent, or one that had clung to grass or weeds touched by the child.

As Ralph, Elsa, and Phil started for the prairie, Ernest Kleinsinger came back.

"Ernest—did you find anything?" his wife cried.

"Nothing, Elsa. Nothing."

The man was haggard, his eyes bloodshot, his voice harsh as a crow's. Turning to Ralph, he said, "Bless you, friend, and the dog who knows more than we do. I will go back to search the prairie with the neighbors as soon as they come."

Out in the grass, Phil trailed behind Ralph and the mother. Every now and then the dog paused to look back wistfully at the house where the gun had been left. He seemed to wonder why a hunter should walk in the prairie without his gun.

Turning once, Ralph saw the first neighbors arriving. They scattered in the thick grass. Cries of "Hanka, Hanka!" from men and women rang across the prairie. There was hardly a chance that the boy could be found by looking. He might have wandered several miles, or he might have fallen asleep, worn out. A searcher could pass within a few yards and not see him.

About a mile from the house, at a spot where the grass was only knee-high, Ralph stopped. He took one of Hanka's socks from his pocket and held it before the dog. "Smell this, Phil. Hanka's sock. Hanka's sock. Go find Hanka, Phil. Go find Hanka!"

The dog sniffed, then studied the man's face as if trying to discover his meaning. Next he trotted straight ahead for a few paces, stopped, and turned around to see if Ralph approved.

"Come here, Phil. Let's try again." Ralph called.

Phil sniffed the sock again, and this time he trotted a little way to the right before turning.

"No, Phil, come back. Smell Hanka's sock. Now go find Hanka."

The dog smelled, quickly ran off to the left, and was called back again. Phil was bewildered. Every direction he had tried was wrong. What was he supposed to do? He dropped his head and tail and walked dejectedly by his master's side.

Ralph and Elsa were far more discouraged than the dog as they trudged on, through the entire morning. Again and again Ralph tried to make Phil understand that he must make big, sweeping circles and zigzags to find the boy that smelled like the sock. He must hunt for the child as he would hunt for a prairie chicken. The dog wanted desperately to please his master, yet he could not comprehend this new kind of hunting.

Once he took Hanka's sock in his mouth and walked proudly, head high, as if to say, "Now I understand. You want me to carry it." But he quickly saw the disappointment in Ralph's face and brought the sock back. Ralph took it, patted the dog sympathetically, and the three moved slowly on through the deep grass.

It was past noon. Not a cloud shielded the searchers from the steady heat of the sun. Ralph and Elsa had not taken time for breakfast, and they carried neither water nor food—except for two biscuits that Elsa had wedged into the pocket of her cotton dress. "Hanka will be hungry," she explained to Ralph.

They were eight miles or more from the Kleinsinger cabin. The search, Ralph believed, was hopeless. Phil did not know what to do, and even if he understood, what chance was there of finding the boy's trail at such a distance? Still, there was no thought of giving up. Ralph was resolved to walk as long as daylight lasted, but he began to worry lest Elsa collapse from exhaustion. She had been on her feet for twenty-four hours.

Suddenly Phil stopped. He sniffed the ground, looked pleased, and began running back and forth as if seeking a warmer scent. The setter looked up at Ralph with bright eyes, then trotted slowly forward, his nose close to the ground.

Ralph and Elsa quickened their steps, each beginning to hope. But the hunter knew it was more likely that Phil had picked up the scent of a prairie chicken or rabbit.

Then the dog paused to lift his elegant nose to a tall weed. This was too high to be brushed by a prairie chicken, and if it had been touched by a deer the sharp hoofs would have left prints in the sod. Nor was it a wolf, for the dog did not have the angry look and the bared teeth that he always showed when he crossed the trail of this enemy.

Phil kept on, scenting every tuft of grass and every flower. Sometimes he stopped and took a long, slow sniff at a certain plant, his eyes half-closed as though the sunlight might interfere with his sense of smell. Ralph watched every move he made. The mother kept close behind, almost stepping on the hunter's heels.

"Is he tracking Hanka?" she asked, over and over. "Will he find him?"

Ralph was not yet certain that the setter was on the boy's trail. But he had never seen Phil act this way when pursuing game.

The track was stale, hard for the setter to follow. Once he lost the scent. He stopped, turned, and made a circle that brought him back to his starting point. But the trail was still lost. Immediately he made a much wider circle, yet it too was a failure. Phil gave one sharp cry of vexation and then tried a different plan. He turned back on his trail, passing Ralph and Elsa, and trotted out of sight.

"We should follow?" the mother asked.

"No," said Ralph. "He has missed a turn somewhere and we'll wait until he finds it. Our footsteps would just mess up the trail."

Soon the dog returned, stepping slowly and cautiously, sniffing the plants to left and right. Less than twenty-five yards from the spot where he had lost the scent he turned off, tail swinging with confidence. Ralph and Elsa came up at a trot to join him.

Now the dog was hurrying. He went a short distance, then checked himself and made a half-turn to examine the stalk of a tall plant he was passing. It was the prairie dock, crowned with yellow ray flowers three inches across, on a level with Ralph's

head. Phil did not look up at the blossoms. His nose went briefly to something that had been caught on the sturdy stalk, two feet above the ground. He glanced at Ralph, eyes shining, as if to ask, "How do you like that?"

Ralph caught his breath. At last there was evidence of what Phil was trailing: a few shreds of blue cotton, torn from a shirt. The blue was deeper, richer, than the shade used in the textile mills of New England. It was a color that might have been home-dyed by a German housewife.

Elsa rushed up and saw instantly what the dog had discovered. "It is Hanka's! I know it is Hanka's!" she cried, snatching the tiny fragment of cloth.

"I think you're right," Ralph agreed. "I've never seen this shade of blue in a Yankee shirt."

Several neighbors appeared on the crest of a nearby ridge.

34

"We've found his trail!" Elsa cried. "We've found his trail!"

The news was relayed across the ocean of grass to more distant searchers and soon a dozen men and women began to push toward Ralph and Elsa. Ernest Kleinsinger was one of the first to reach them.

Phil paid no attention to the crowd. He had work to do with his delicate nose and he hurried on, fringed tail swinging. Ralph called back to the neighbors, "Keep to the side of the dog's trail! He may lose the scent and have to go back!"

The prairie pioneers understood. They strode through the grass to the left and right of Phil's path.

The setter had become a different dog. His tail no

longer drooped, his head did not hang in failure. He had learned at last what Ralph wanted and he was proud of his success. But there was difficult work ahead, for the trail was cold and could not be followed fast. Every plant and clump of grass had to be smelled.

For more than two hours, while the sun wheeled down toward the horizon, the farm people tramped behind the brown and white setter. Often the tall grass hid the dog from everyone except Ralph and the Kleinsingers.

Phil worked with his mouth open to get air for his lungs. He saved his nose for smelling, since the delicate nerves told him more with just a gentle whiff of air.

Emerging from the grass, Phil stepped onto an old buffalo track, still a dusty trail. And there Ralph saw something that he tried to hide from Elsa. It was the print of a child's bare foot, so clear that the weary mother might get hysterical if she saw it. Such a commotion could interrupt Phil and delay the search, already much too late.

The hunter thought fast. Quickly he put his own foot over the small print. But Elsa noticed the movement, and she also had made a discovery—another print of a small foot in a dusty spot, just ahead.

"It's Hanka's! It's Hanka's!" she cried. "He must be near!"

Ralph caught her arm as she darted forward. "Keep to one side," he cautioned. Then he squatted to examine the second track with a hunter's skill. After a long minute he spoke.

"No, I'm afraid he isn't near. Look what happens when I blow on this track." He puffed and his breath swept some of the dust outlining the foot into the air.

"You see? This print was made yesterday afternoon, when the dust had been dried by the sun. If it had been made this morning, while the dust was still

covered with dew, the print would have been firm. I couldn't have blown away the dust as I did."

"But maybe Hanka passed by only a little while ago, when the dust was dry."

Ralph pointed to the twisting track left by a worm that had crawled across the footprint.

"That is the trail of a slow-worm. Sometimes it travels only a few feet in an hour. Let's see how far it has gone."

Ten yards ahead they found the worm, almost a foot long and covered with glassy scales. It was snaking its way along the buffalo track, searching for earthworms and slugs. Probably several hours had passed since the worm had crossed Hanka's footprint.

The hunter was certain that Hanka's trail was a day old. The child might be miles away, unless he had fallen from exhaustion or had been discovered by wolves. But Ralph kept his fears to himself.

"It was Hanka's track, I am sure," he told Elsa and Ernest. "However, I think we have some distance to go." Then, turning to the neighbors who were closing in, he shouted, "Keep a stone's throw behind us! Don't get close to the dog!"

Deeply absorbed in his task, Phil was well ahead

on the buffalo trail. The dog moved slowly, for it was hard to smell a track in dry dust. Yet Phil signaled his confidence with every wide swing of his tail. His nose swung too, as he sniffed the grass along the path to catch any scent left by the boy's hands or clothes.

The trail led across several low ridges and skirted marshlands between the hills. At the top of one small hill a gopher had piled up dirt a foot high. Phil stopped to sniff the mound, which had been packed flat on top by Hanka's bare feet. The toes pointed in all directions. Evidently the boy had stood on this high spot, turning to north, east, south, and west, looking for a cabin that was more than ten miles away. But all he could have seen was one ridge after another, each covered with waving grass.

Halfway down the mound Ralph noticed the prints of heels. They showed that the frightened child had sat down, perhaps to cry, perhaps to wonder where to go next.

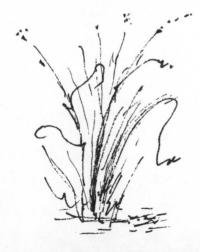

Phil had sniffed the buffalo trail well beyond the mound without finding Hanka's scent. He came back at a brisk trot and made a narrow circle around the gopher's earthworks. Picking up the scent in another direction, he headed into the grass. Here he could track the boy much faster than in the dust. He traveled so swiftly that only Ralph and the Kleinsingers kept up with him.

The dog led them down a hill to a little brook that flowed between low banks lined with alders. At the water's edge he halted. There was a splash as a frog leaped from a mossy stone into a small pool. Ignoring the frog, Phil kept his nose to the ground and retraced his steps for a few yards.

Elsa reached the brook just as the dog turned away. She gave a low scream, but quickly covered her mouth. In the wet earth at her feet were the deep imprints of Hanka's hands where he had lowered his mouth to the water. After drinking, the boy had started back toward the hill, then changed his direction.

Phil stood for a moment at the spot where the child had turned. His nose was pointed toward a clump of elderberry bushes a short way up the stream. Suddenly the dog raised his head higher and stretched his neck forward. He marched straight ahead with deliberate steps, no longer sniffing, no longer swinging his tail. Ralph knew instantly that Phil had scented the boy himself, wherever he lay hidden.

Elsa saw the change, too. "He has left off hunting!" she cried in dismay. Then, remembering how Phil had behaved while stalking game, she understood. "He has found him!"

She made a frantic dash past the dog to the elderberry bushes, her husband close behind. Ralph stood frozen. There was a terrible chance that the parents would find only what the wolves had left. But there was no mistaking the cry of joy a moment later, a cry that made Hanka wake up with a terrified scream.

Phil and Ralph sprinted to the bushes where Elsa had the boy in her arms. Tears poured down her face.

"Is he all right?" Ralph asked.

Half-sobbing, half-laughing, Elsa could only nod her head. She fumbled for one of the biscuits. Ernest pulled out a big red handkerchief and wiped his nose. Then he wiped the faces of his wife and the wailing child.

Hanka's blond curls were snarled. His shirt front was streaked with dirt and sweat and one sleeve was torn. His face and hands were stained purple from elderberries, the only food he had tasted in almost thirty hours. Beneath an elderberry bush the grass was matted down where he had been sleeping.

Phil cut loose with a frenzied outburst. First he leaped upon Ralph, got a quick pat, and then raced over to Hanka. Standing up with his forepaws against Elsa, he rubbed his nose against the boy's face and hands, then dashed back to Ralph for another pat. Hearing new voices, the dog tore down the path to welcome the first neighbors and escort them to Hanka. Indeed, Phil seemed to think that Hanka now belonged to him. He rubbed against the child again, frisked over to Ralph, and sped off to greet more of the searchers.

Within a few minutes the little band of searchers had assembled by the stream. Hanka, his mouth full of biscuit, stared at the circle around him and finally spoke.

"Let's go home."

Laughter rippled across the prairie for the first time. Home was what everyone wanted. But first the searchers went down on their bellies by the brook, sucking up the cool water, then gathering handfuls to throw against their sweaty faces.

The sun was almost touching the far-off grass as the homeward parade began. Ralph led the way, with Phil by his side except for frequent trips down the line to make sure that Hanka was not lost again. The men took turns carrying the worn-out child.

After traveling three miles with the crowd, Ralph said good-by. He had reached a short cut across the prairie that would bring him to his cabin before dark.

"Oh, Mr. Stark!" Elsa cried. "How can I thank you?" Instantly she found a way. She reached up to the tall, lean hunter, pulled down his head, and kissed him. Ralph blushed, while the men laughed.

"I guess Phil deserved that kiss, ma'am," Ralph said.

As the party moved away, Phil stood motionless, his

eyes fixed on the yellow head bobbing behind the dark hair of Ernest Kleinsinger. Ralph reached down to the setter. "Don't worry, Phil. You'll see him tomorrow when I go for my gun."

The two walked on for a mile before Ralph spoke again.

"Phil, you never told me you were part bloodhound."

The fringed tail made an extra-wide swing.

ALEXANDER L. CROSBY is a former newspaperman and has been a free-lance writer since 1944. *Go Find Hanka!*, his eleventh book for young people, reflects his interest in the history of the frontier—an interest which led him to explore many miles of the old Oregon and California trails while researching an earlier book. Mr. Crosby was born in Catonsville, Maryland, but grew up in California and is a graduate of the University of California at Berkeley. He now lives on a thirty-three acre farm near Quakertown, Pennsylvania, with his wife, Nancy Larrick. Other books by Alexander L. Crosby include *Steamboat Up the Colorado*, *The Rimac, River of Peru*, *The World of Rockets* and *The Junior Science Book of Pond Life*.

GLEN ROUNDS is a man familiar with the wide open spaces of this country. Born in the South Dakota Badlands and brought up on a ranch in Montana, he set out as a young man to "prowl the country" and managed to cover just about all of it. During his wanderings he found time to study art at the Kansas City Art Institute and, later, at the Art Students' League in New York. Mr. Rounds' first book, *Ole Paul, The Mighty Logger*, was published in 1936. Since then he has written and illustrated more than twenty-five books for young people and his illustrations have enlivened dozens of books by other authors. He now lives in Southern Pines, North Carolina.